ROSANGELA LUDOVICO

cathemerals

*To my wife Denise*

**The author:**
Rosangela Ludovico, illustrator, author, and web designer.
Born in 1990 in Castellaneta, Italy.
This book aside, she's actually a very cheerful person.

Contact: rosangelaludovico@gmail.com
Website: http://cyborgize.it

© 2016 Rosangela Ludovico. All rights reserved.
ISBN 978-0-9976871-0-1

1 · rain dancers

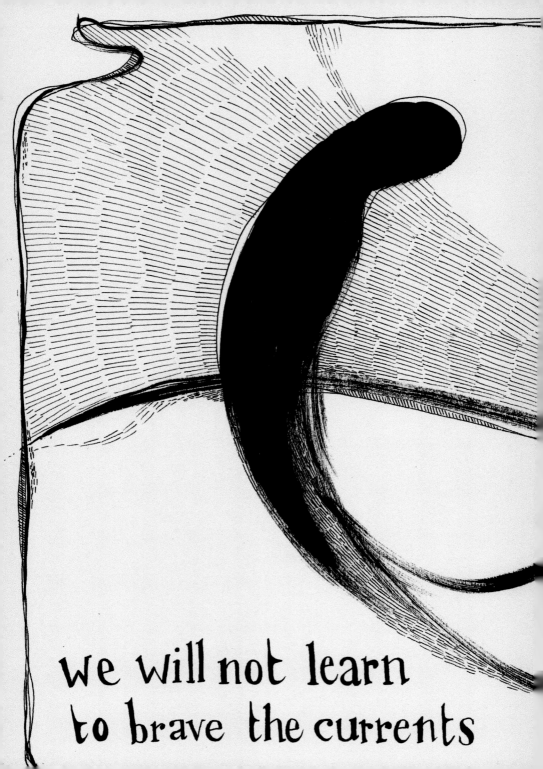

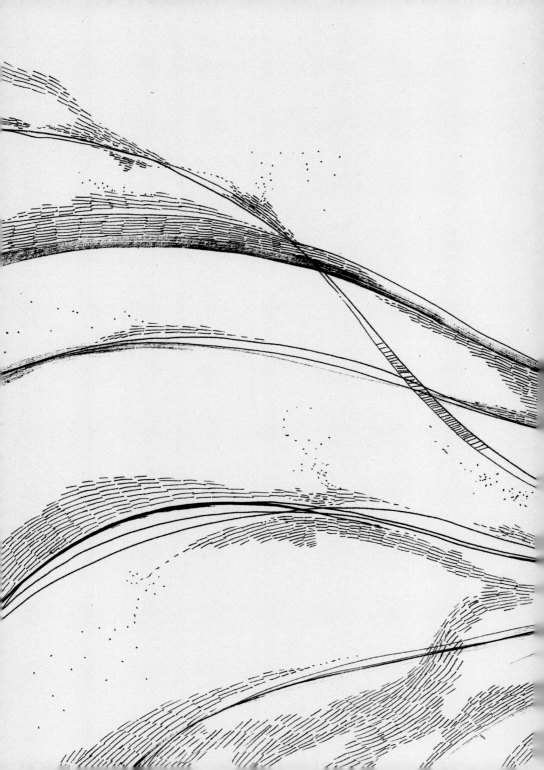

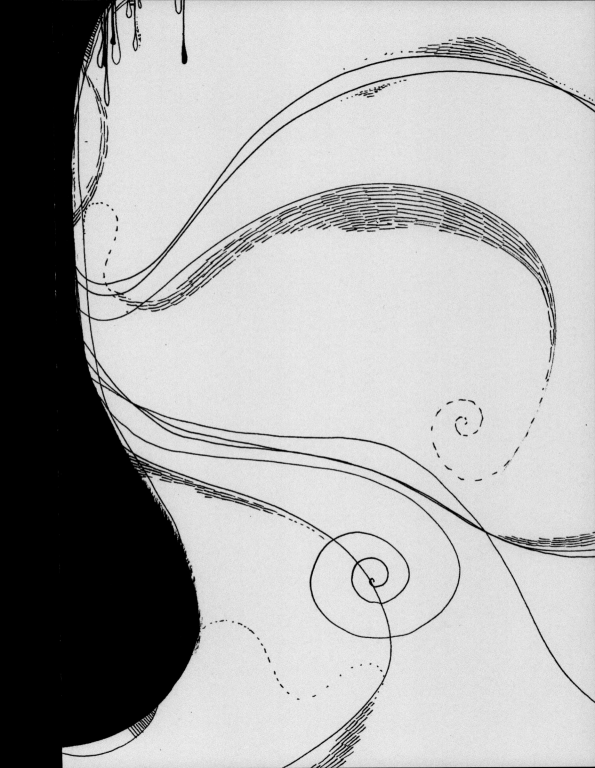

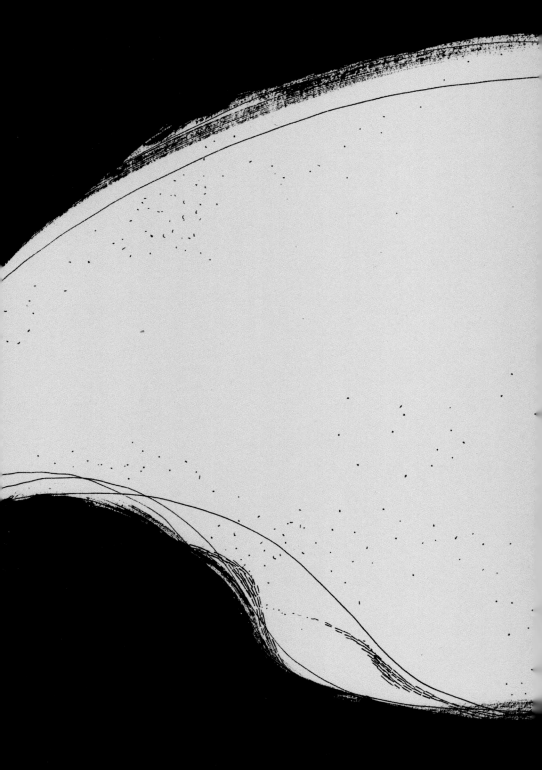

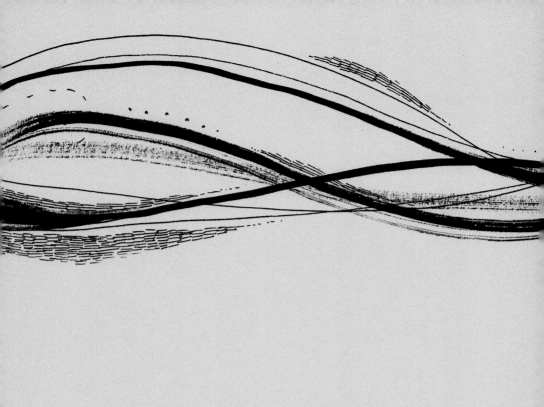

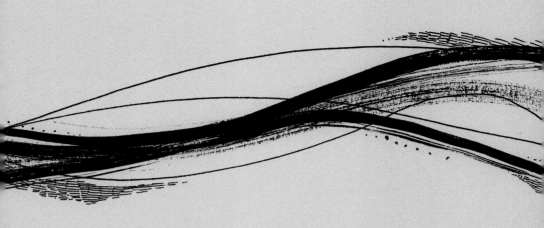

if you hold my hand
we will not drown

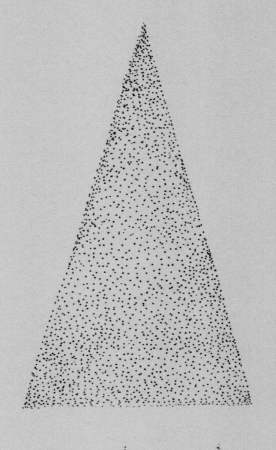

2 . dust

unexpected,
the light surfaces
through dirty windows

reveals
clouds of dust

# a desert of abandoned flesh

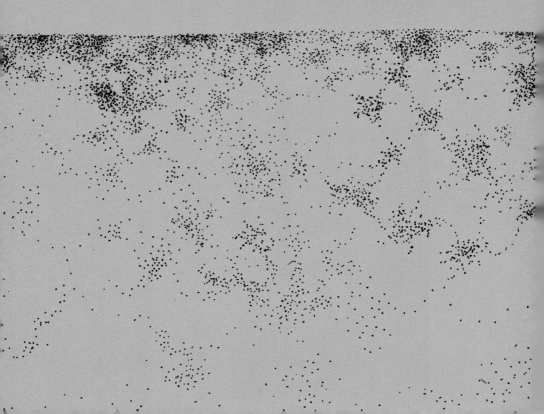

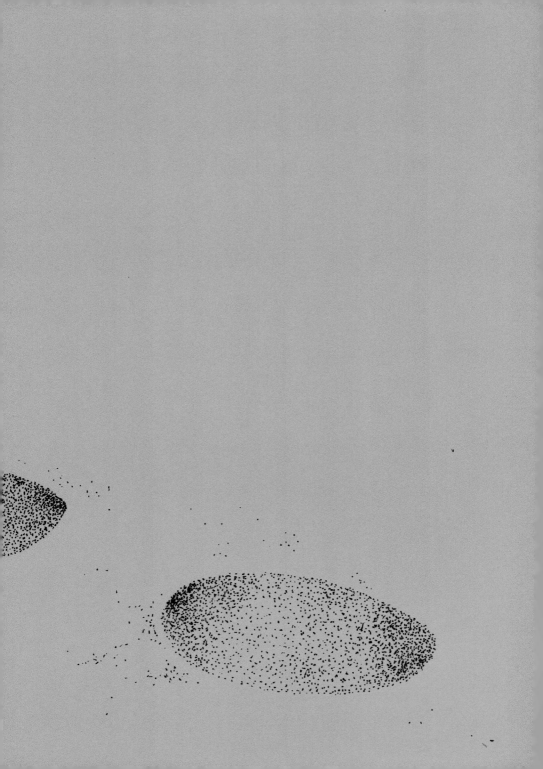

unwanted speckles left behind by a former self

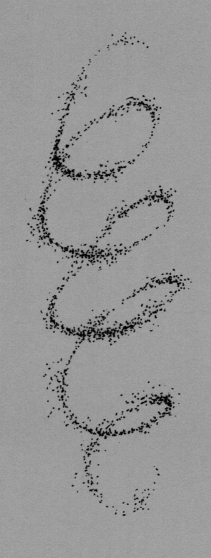

a chrysalis

for every present

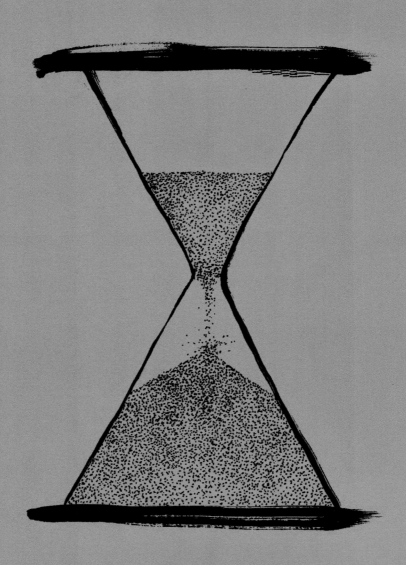

it is futile
to erase
the traces of our death
from here

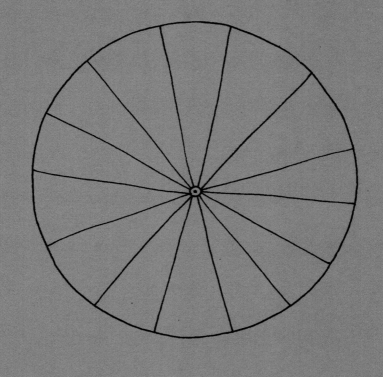

# about that bicycle carcass chained to a pole

missing a wheel,
missing a seat

rusted beyond recognition

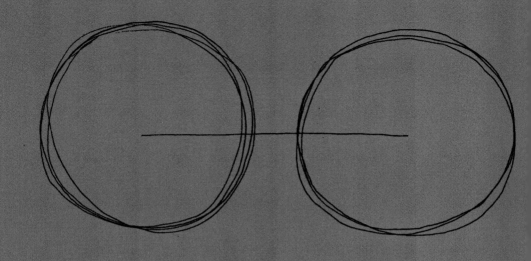

decay claimed it

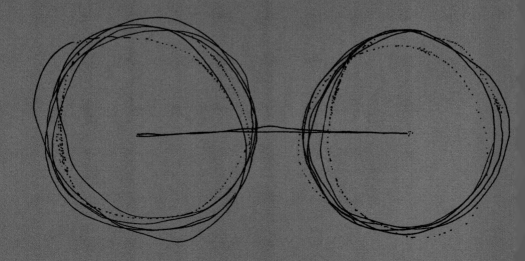

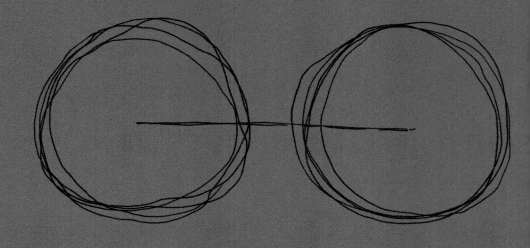

before anyone could

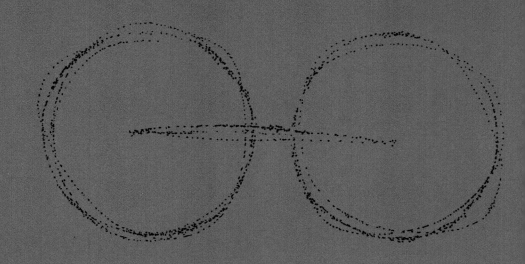

I don't despair

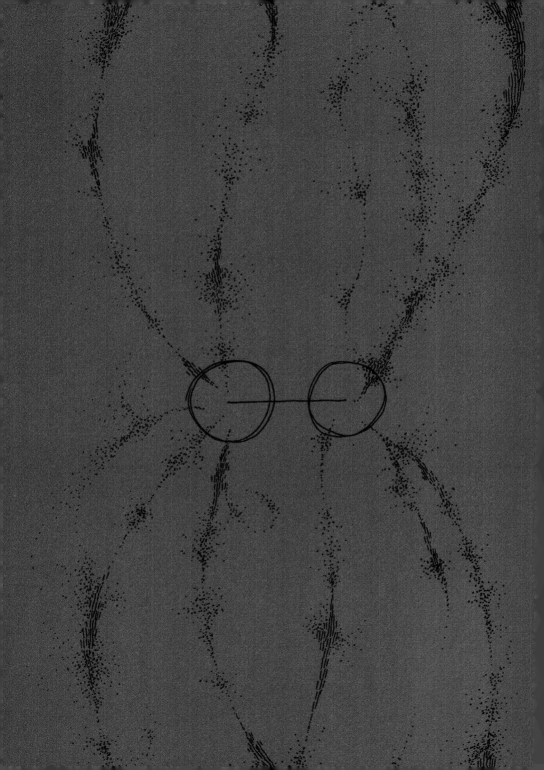

for I can't know
my chains

chasing
suspended

drawing
circles of wings

they balance
above

they came with one wind

and will leave with another

they see
the earth
but once:

in their evening,
the swifts
cry

their ropes
come undone

the earth
reclaims them

5 · orion

in the city's perpetual day

I had forgotten
what was the sky

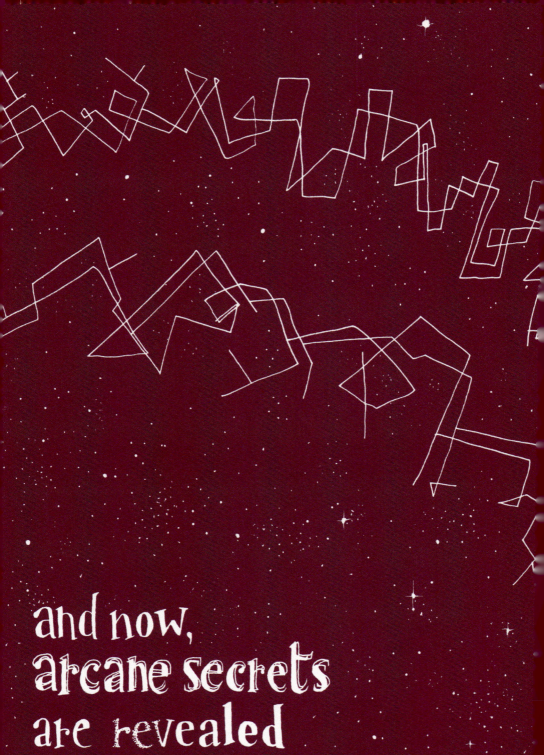

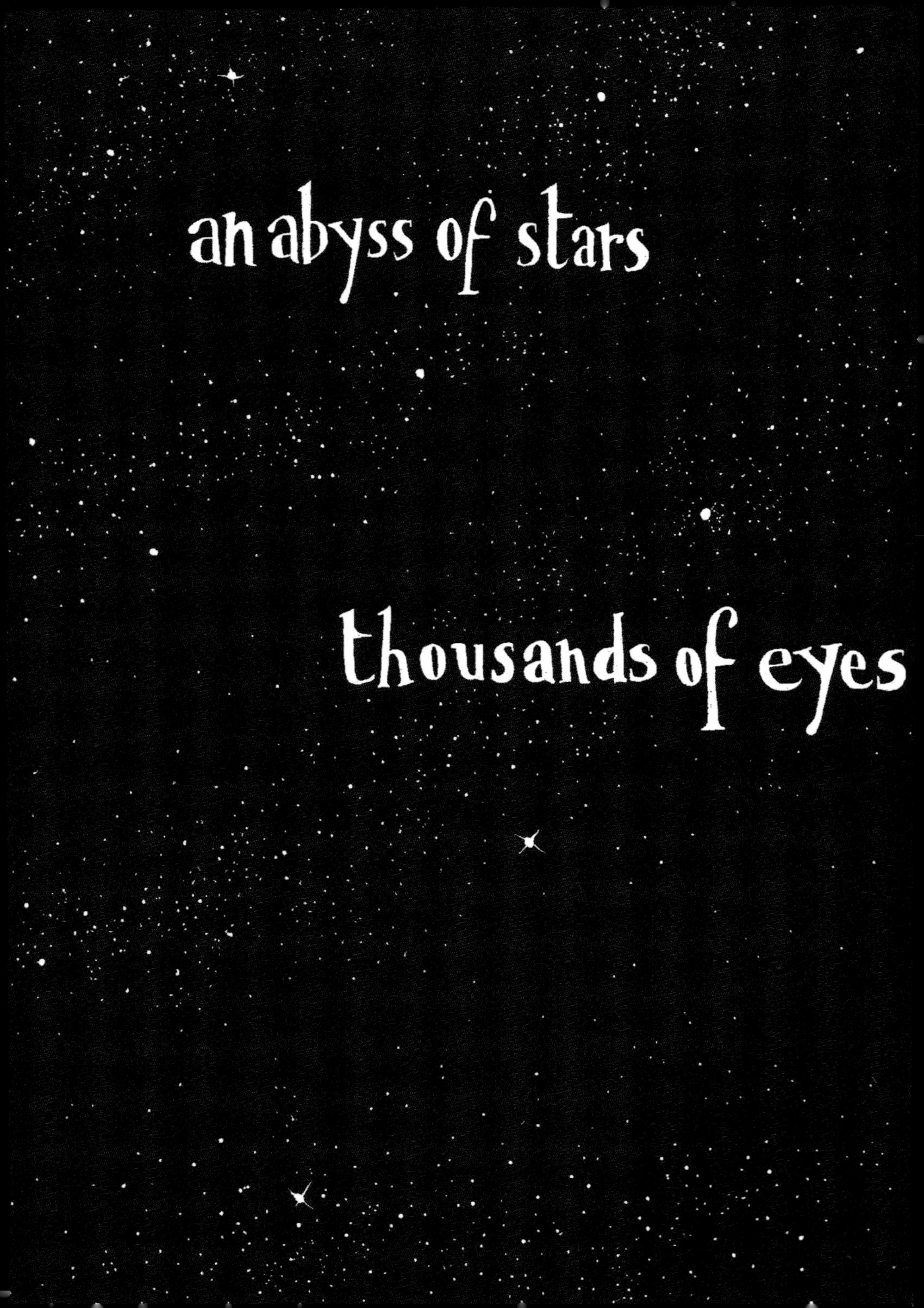

an abyss of stars

thousands of eyes

staring

frozen in the depth
of time

orion
is nowhere
to be found

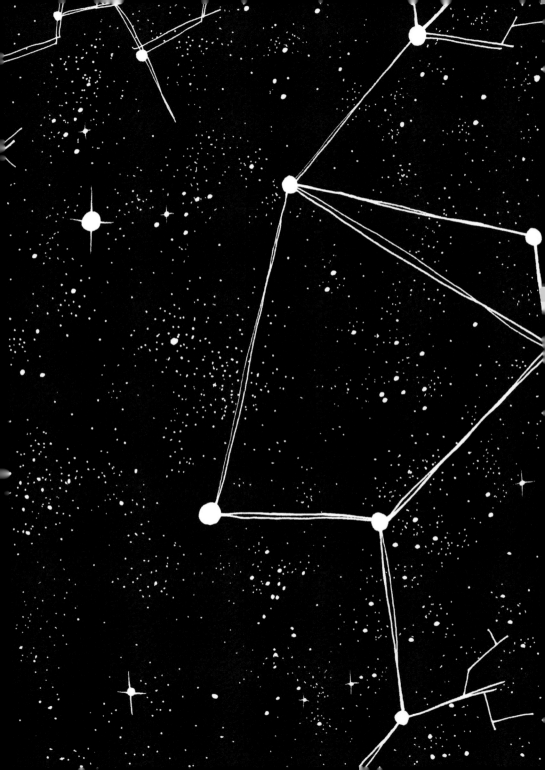

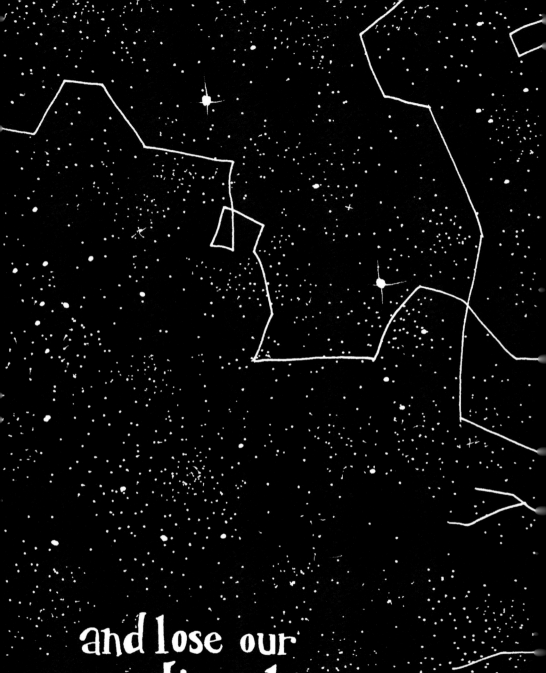

6. the drowning

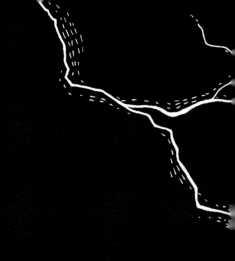

cracks in the walls
appear when you don't know

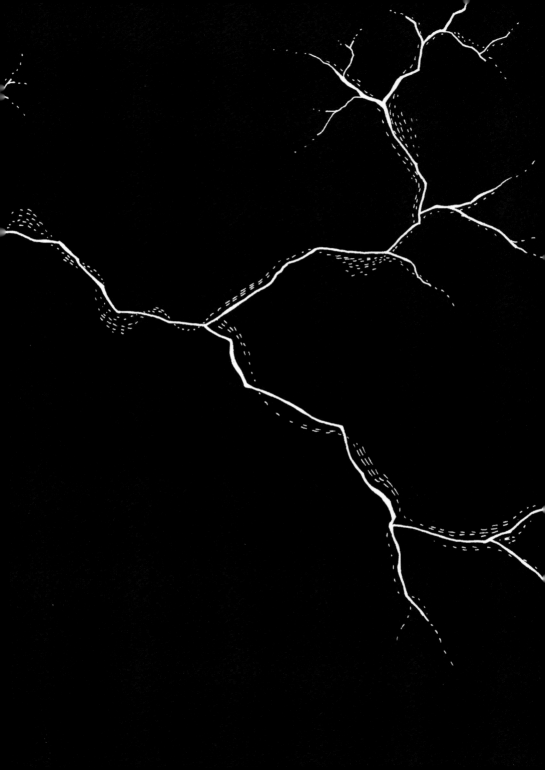

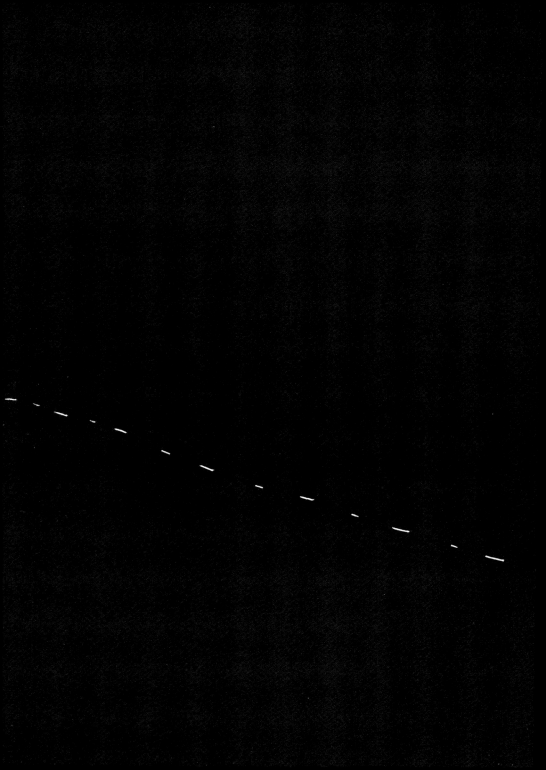

I am afraid

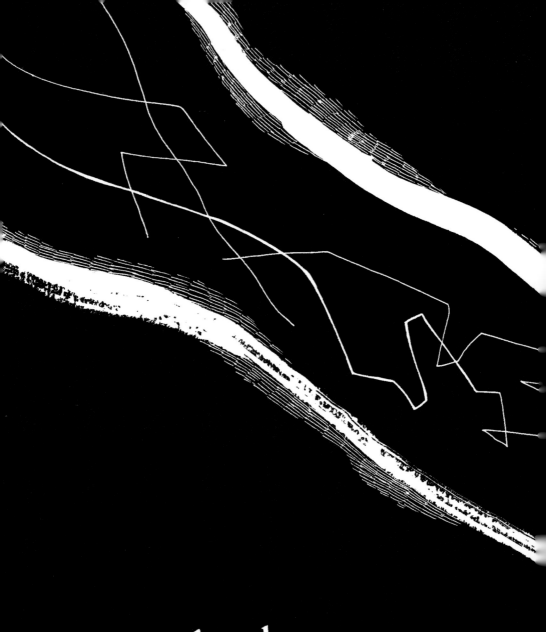

in which the pain
is just as unexpected

will it wear off
or readjust into itself

a malady
of the being
that starves
the self

the night
is at its darkest
before dawn

so I'll wait
for you
to wake up

wake up,

and drown with me